Hypothesis

ALSO BY JOHN BARTON

A Poor Photographer
Hidden Structure
West of Darkness: Emily Carr, a Self-Portrait
Great Men
Notes Toward a Family Tree
Designs from the Interior
Sweet Ellipsis

CHAPBOOKS

Destinations, Leaving the Map
Oxygen
Shroud

EDITOR

Silences
belles lettres / beautiful letters
We All Begin in a Little Magazine: Arc and the Promise
of Canada's Poets, 1978–1998 (with Rita Donovan)

John Barton

Hypothesis

Poems

Published in 2001 in Canada and in 2002 in the United States by
House of Anansi Press Limited
895 Don Mills Rd., 400-2 Park Centre
Toronto, ON M3C 1W3
Tel. (416) 445-3333
Fax (416) 445-5967
www.anansi.ca

Distributed in Canada by
General Distribution Services Ltd.
325 Humber College Blvd.
Etobicoke, ON M9W 7C3
Tel. (416) 213-1919
Fax (416) 213-1917
E-mail cservice@genpub.com

Distributed in the United States by
General Distribution Services Inc.
PMB 128, 4500 Witmer Industrial Estates
Niagara Falls, NY 14305-1386
Toll Free Tel. 1-800-805-1083
Toll Free Fax 1-800-481-6207
E-mail gdsinc@genpub.com

05 04 03 02 01   1 2 3 4 5

CANADIAN CATALOGUING IN PUBLICATION DATA

Barton, John, 1957–
Hypothesis

ISBN 0-88784-659-9

I. Title.

PS8553.A78H95 2001   C811'.54   C00-933198-0
PR9199.3.B37H95 2001

Editor: Erin Mouré
Cover design: Angel Guerra
Cover photo: Hugh Travers
Typesetting: Brian Panhuyzen
Printed and bound in Canada

THE CANADA COUNCIL | LE CONSEIL DES ARTS
FOR THE ARTS | DU CANADA
SINCE 1957 | DEPUIS 1957

We acknowledge for their financial support of our publishing program the Canada
Council for the Arts, the Ontario Arts Council, and the Government of Canada
through the Book Publishing Industry Development Program (BPIDP).

for Philip and Bill

Where is here?

— Northrop Frye

There is no person without a world.

— Anne Carson

Contents

I

Watershed

Everywhere the blue and green world.

Your button-down shirt and corduroys.

The disparate shores of the park joined by opposed lanes
of traffic above the river below, the currents
of noise and moving

lights on the bridge easing as we enter the cloudy
starred bowl turned over the park's laconic
band shell, the banks

of the torrent we walk along
thrown wide, the open

neck of your shirt
disclosing a weedy insinuation

of chest hair, the copper-green veins of your throat, and aspen
coloured eyes looking downward, stirring the cold
backwaters of mine.

While a blue heron lifts greyly from the bird sanctuary
mallards with matte malachite
heads alight beside us in a moonstruck eddy
of rushes, assumed processional one or two swim away from

each season, away from the cycle
of the arbitrary, webbed
feet feyly waving *adieu* like we do (or

is it "hello"?)

Hello, stranger, hello —

Against the riverine sheets of my bed the frontiers
of your body exposed with
dexterity

terrain not undisturbed before we met but still something I want
to attend to and tend — the very pith of you
sunburned, hay-stubbled, cicada-lyred, unfenced-in

ground some would call waste

renewing itself, delirious, verdant
humours rising
to my fingers, your bracken

patterned olive and bice

boxers large and loose upon your hips, tongue
leafing into mouth, timothy
sage, kinnikinnick —

this bed a raft of green, fresh-cut
logs shot
forward by the snow
melt of my for-now exhausted blues through

a city where some of us
grow afraid of
adding
                    nothing to the flow

but you say
we take nothing away

so without issue despite the love we commit.

We are living the new equations
of this aqueous
arboreal enlightenment.

Somewhere in the open water
of Hudson Bay, blue
is the hue of the future, millennial, a blue

ravished planet set

adrift in the heavens and seen
from afar, our fellow
men swept up in its whirl, perspectives over

whelmed in the greenwood beneath the azure
foreknowing
of dawn, their consciousness up close and engorged.

So the green body calms the blue mind
briefly — still one reminds
the other of
its place in the whole.

Decline and regeneration are everywhere.

Everywhere the blue and green world.

Hypothesis

Because positive was negative
because his body
was too full of antibodies

he let in

the cells of a baboon protected
by nature from whatever

makes him sick, killing him slowly
but still too fast.
He won't

go quietly

he says, he won't let any
one forget, his
body

a memorial in the making
to the other

men already gone, to the positive
men of the future, to the ones
who don't yet know, his will bodacious

unlike his nearly exhausted
T-cells so far

still

able to fight the routine, opportunistic
illnesses of the soul
his positivity has invited in.

Though he wants to be negative
it's not in his nature
anymore to

be anything *less*.

Because positive was negative
the baboon was killed
its resistant
cells tentative inside him, resident

aliens.

Are these the foreign agents every
body fears?
Their rumoured
inhumanity might already

covertly circulate among us.
Some panic

the secrets of the flesh we are
beginning to unlock
too easily

let in the future
the cells

of an animal sampled
by those who kill
because they have no choice

because they require a specimen
for further study, data
to write up

once

they have risked everything to
turn something positive
negative
their careers

suspended in the blood of a man
who took chances
in bed he recognized

too late, the trust between lovers
a probability except
by intuition
even doctors at one time had no

reason to doubt.
The scientific method.

Those ethical, clean
cut guys
in lab coats, they look nervous.
They find it hard

to be objective, are trained to
be optimistic
but feel left out

by anyone with a positive
attitude who has
learned, with sacrifice, to keep all

affirmation to himself.

Palm Springs

why swim through the clear
waters of those who remain
thirsty, exhausting the lowered
reservoirs of your strength, the aquifers too
quickly drained far

beneath the continent, cavernous
hearts half empty and ignored

unreplenished below
this spreading city where stinging
treated water is stirred by arms and legs
and a torso, perspiring, you contrive
to move in toned
sculpted harmonies

your butterfly accelerating, lap
after lap, over the startled
surface of the pool, effortless

random stone skidding
across the endless imminence
of sinking, a fool's
kind of immortality, until
the reservoirs of your strength
of their own

accord, exhaust
themselves and the body
thirsts, parched

wells sunk
without thought deeper than can be guessed
below the surprised, irrigated, suddenly
saline wastes of the imagination
whose forced

bloom has begun to hang
anemic on the espaliered
vine, the aging body a planet
in denial where from the beginning
water is neither

created nor destroyed, but now
no longer falls in plentitude
or fresh, the unforeseen
subsidences you would today lament
were your desire

not a river diverted
or dammed, its infernal course, straightened
and constrained, made to wander
away from

glacier and mouth, unable to mingle
its silty origins in the rising
oceans where all streams in time
were once recurrently supposed

to expire, but instead what
remains of the flow
pools at some far and temporary
oasis where men
swim in unison, said to be
beautiful and impossible
to leave

Phone Lines

Voicelessness —

and then, circumspectly
there are too many

inside the head and
out, sound
bytes spliced into this *a capella*

choir, each one of us
a soloist who just

had to call in, desires
inharmonic

and randomly
arranged
ad hominem, voices

multiplying
dividing

like cells whenever
receivers all
through

the night are put down
gently or picked

up and cradled
dial

tones at last   broken

or not; the dark's
dimension
-less silence a gap — *agapé* — (this

brotherly love) yours

one more voice in the night
its wilderness

sped

by Telus Mobility deep
into the body
through

the ear in

to the anonymous orbit of
another's distant
desire
the body your voice is: skin

bruised by touch

tone numbers unfelt
fingers
depress, ciphers each one

of us, not so
sweet the zeros

sad solitude makes us

give voice to, leaving
the data
trace our bodyscapes come

quickly to be known
by, all switches

in the receptor

brain

thrown and synesthetic — hair
suddenly *hazel*, eyes
ebony-hard
the lip's quicksilver remoteness

licorice, quince, radicchio —

self-reflexive arias unsated
by the heat
scored
profanely into the heart by an

other

's — (*my/your*) — degraded circuitry, phone
lines
connecting to

only disconnect —

all voices safely erased.

At Lindow

I found you
    among the mosses beyond the airport where new
      runway landing lights lead to
        arrival

        the excavated layers
    of peat revealing you
  slumped forward, head pitched slightly
to the right
        against your shoulder
    naked, torso

    misshaped by cumulations
yards thick, legs
  missing, but only one
        foot, ginger beard matted, a band of fox
    fur round what is left
of your forearm, skin leathery, but smooth, tobacco
    hued, cured
      by centuries

      of tannins in the dripping
        sphagnum, a wound reopening

        in the neck where we touched
as you were brought to
  light, blood
    long ago emptied

    not into this watery
  cold, almost airless
acidic bog

not flowing like traffic that now seldom
    drains completely from nearby
        roadways at night beneath stars no one
            local will much longer know the names of

            but collected
        instead in some now absent
sacred vessel, the garrotte stopping breath
    bleeding to and from
            your lungs still knotted
        thrice, savage, taut

        about your neck, the skull's
base and crown a record
    of the three grave axe blows blessing you while
            you knelt, mistletoe

            an aftershock hinted at
        in the gut down through
time of the libation
    you drank, airborne
            pollens you ingested with a burnt
        oatcake reminding me it was

        spring when we met, this black
    pool then pristine
remote
    limitless, my body the whole unrecoverable
        disenfranchised generations
            since, carried

           forward reincarnate beyond
       Lindow Moss's vigorous
diminishment, your chest caved in round nothing
           where belief once
     surfaced, what ribs

   remaining, soft as prophesy in the margins
           of the bog, silent
                   witness to its retreat while transatlantic
flights touch down, your body devoted
           given over

       unlike mine has ever been, sacrificed
lover, to the release of what is
     now waning moss, cotton grass
           and ling

Oxygen

Fuselage sloughed like skin of a burn victim.

Brutal, mute.

Broken wing dragging on the flinty tarmac as our plane
goes down —
                    now: the sudden
                                        lacuna
of how we've come
to walk away, luggageless

unscathed, left to stand intact amid the smouldering
fields in the raw

air, calm — the content

of who we are
                    torn asunder, falling
                                        across the unfamiliar
dusk-bled
suburbs below our flight path.

As always, what serves to destroy us saves us — thrown
clear, flown
                    far too quickly toward this
pause — oxygen
sucked
out of us, airframe exploding

something ripe against the ground, the appalling

technology freeing
                    astonished
amnesiacs.
            Time stands still as we stand still
momentarily eternal

grateful
for the emergencies dashed at our feet.

Transient

under torn ozone you repack
your nurse's black bag now transformed
        into a 30-pound knapsack, its contents
            shouldered, expanded

    out of necessity — space
blankets since on the street there are never enough
        sleeping bags; granola bars, because everyone is
            hungry — the night ward you care for

    too many more blocks of the city
than you can walk, spread beyond the core where gusts
        of the wind are glancing and also
            without stars, those who feel hopelessly

    chilled you find under the dank span
of the bridge, east of downtown
        not far from the zoo, whatever they need you try
            to give, the little you have

    you set down in the open by the dark
mountain-fed river, fast-flowing
        and slowly undrinkable, the hospital on the farther
            bank recently collapsed

    in a controlled implosion out
of which cranes for the new
        condominiums now tower, overlooking the empty
            park where dinosaurs cast

    from concrete feed in a simulacrum
of the transient world that one day
        would betray them, the prehistoric grown
            suddenly cool

while the condoms you distribute are
temporary succour against more than one
                    discharged contagion, though not anymore
                         do you try to contain

the fallout of what spreads
inside bodies and out — lungs that should never have
                    gone tubercular, cuts
                         going septic — you can't

help them, your knapsack so heavy
yet empty, its contents your hands have become, offering
                    not cures, but chance
                         ways of coping, roofs made

from cardboard, held
aloft with duct tape, your makeshift
                    structures soon collapsing in the rain
                         on the bodies

of those who seek warmth in each
other's arms, fighting off another
                    sleep whose embrace some swoon
                         into easily, brought on

by snows drifting about their entanglement
so early in the season, flurries loosed
                    on them, ash befallen the dinosaurs after
                         an asteroid's nightmare

encounter with the Earth, clouds weighting
the atmosphere with a cold whose torpor
                    too few of us you feel have come to fear
                         too few ever wake from

Chrysaora

Monterey Bay Aquarium, October 1999

        heartless shape
            shifters — cumulus
rinsed through and aqueous
       with early light, now barely
          orange, adrift

           without thought in
        arhythmic slumbering
currents of plankton, each sea nettle a directionless
        astral storm of pure
           hunger less body than

             ghost — transparent desire
     far and long ago from
         shore, in galaxies feeding
in azure about to deepen ageless
      past

         dusk toward night, the sea's
            abysmal
dreams sensed only
        through absences of conscious
           surface light, the jellies' eyeless

            novas prehensile as the winged antennas
     of satellites, the invisible
stinging tentacles distending from speechless
         gelid bells unrepentant
     as the voracious

       webs of gravity
          exploded stars
unloose, spider-like, from cooling mael
       stroms of the bottom
         less

Shroud

There are no pockets in the shroud.
— Edmund White

The Living Room

Their rubbish alone was left.
He was a vacant lot,
he had become an exemption.
The squares of his mind were empty.
— P. K. Page, "In Memoriam"

At the drop-in clinic near the centre
of town, I namelessly drop off
cotton shirts wrinkled as grey skin
to be slung on hangers and rifled through
by men whose flesh thins under the shaking
force of their scapulae, the deft
articulation of fingers a memory
as they thumb through gaunt fabric —
the colours so bereft
their rubbish alone was left.

Even as I drive away, a man buttons
wash-worn cotton about his body
as it vanishes, ribs rising through
jaundiced skin like stains as he breathes
haltingly, or so I think, driving away
with my fears intact, overwrought
about whatever might or might not be
deadly in my own blood, haunted
by my one parting thought:
He was a vacant lot.

Against my will, I slip inside
his flesh. Its slim vitality sits
amply on my shoulders as I drive uptown
every remaining bit of pleasure to be
had from it an undiscovered country
lying within reach, vague satisfaction
of desires unable to die
with him, the body a cairn, fog
lifting as I pause at an intersection.
He had become an exemption.

His world opens up: his death is my death
his love my love, the men he kissed
and held are men like us who've passed
through the ordinary arms of several others
dates in loose cotton shirts who drove us
home after the movies, each entreaty
to love made on nights when warmth was wanted.
Guys who made us feel safe not cautious.
One foolhardy night he fleetingly felt free.
The squares of his mind were empty.

Prêt-à-Porter

You want to let him

take you shopping for clothes
but you are afraid: these
dangerous
                    off-the-rack
love affairs quickly
come to wear you
out, but
                    I tell you when
the body is sick
this is what he needs

a chance

to spoil you (not with the virus —
for he grows

more fearful of its invisible
dropped stitches
each time your bodies join —

but) with the illusion
he has time

on his hands, though in the end
whatever he might buy you
may well hang
at the back of your closet alongside
those tasteful, uncomfortably
white shirts you've kept.

Who can resist

gifts wrapped in the water
marked tissues
of the most exclusive haberdashers?

The worked fabric of the virgin
wool suit he has
long had his eye on —

its twill no less
soft to the cheek and golden
than the fine hairs on his thighs —

will wear more
slowly thin than the dead

layer of skin you wash from his back
whenever he is
lonely and nakedly in need

of the tenderness you give
without question, cock
hardening against his spine, arms folding
him closer in the shower, lost

in the mist.
Though you've come

to know him in a short time
only, how
to tell him this

is what you want: the moment

stripped of the unstable
accoutrements
about to haunt dresser drawers, the future

dispossessed of any unwelcome
monogrammed cufflinks
whose sole
purpose is to tarnish at the wrist?

Behind tonight's drawn

curtain of steam and running
water, its sly white
noise whispering sweet nothings until the water
runs cold, you ask him to

caress your body
to clothe it
with pleasures only the weave
of his tongue can tease out, lingering
over your nipples, the flushed pink
sheen of your stomach —
the soul immune

to the changing fashions
of the flesh
your lucent, his waning skin.

Plasma, Triangles of Silk

the shirt you gave me I passed on to a friend, yellow silk the colour
of plasma, too soon worn out by years of wear and cut when needed

into triangles sewn by hand with a running stitch to other salvaged
bits of fabric forming squares joined into blocks then rows assembled

strip by strip, the pattern of the quilt revealing the care behind it the way
the shirt no longer can, my favourite shirt, given to heal something

between us in ways the year that tore us apart never could, a shirt
despite everything I wore thin with love, wore almost daily, loose-fitting

and cool to the skin while all around us men were dying, men we did
not know and read about in the paper, men like us, bodies full of a virus

no one at first understood was making copies of itself in their blood
perfect copies made from enzymes we now know, after thousands died

how to starve the virus of, years spent piecing together an erratic if ever
more exacting model of how it disperses through the body, its dark hold

on the imagination at last worn through but not wholly gone, the still
lethal viral load like the metaphors of plague lowered to levels

undetectable in the blood, the triangles of plasma-coloured silk entrusted
to a slowly apparent design, each one cut expressly like the other

then positioned in arcane patterns to catch the eye through variation
and distract it from their wavering abundance, the triangles unrecognizable

except by us to be from a shirt I once wore to know myself by, a single
man who otherwise might have put on a future time could not alter

its unchosen motifs the possibilities still underpinning my life: the virus
able to kill, as always — yet today we read some men forget, joining

their bodies without protection, unmindful the porous, spontaneous
membranes between them are still thinner than silk, the now exposed

patterns of contagion unchanged from the start unlike the treatments
multiplying by trial and error, the dissemblings of the virus so many

scientists work hard to pin down, but they have yet to get everything
precisely right, always aware the triangles of whatever cloth, seam

by seam, must be picked apart with care, the design discovered to be
wanting, not good enough, though the bits thrown aside may point to

how else they might be joined, the coherence searched for perhaps
made up from what is not recognized in what already seems to

be known though a cure will never bring back the dead, it should unravel
the evidence they left us in the blood, painfully ripped-out threads read

by anyone who does not want to pass their message on, the quilt stitched
with quiet knowing hands toward something no less bold in design than

the shirt: silk the colour of plasma, of inspiration, its triangulation never
once undoing your gift, a contagious, heartfelt gesture that healed us both

Body Bag

The results came back
negative and already I am

beginning not to remember your name
its syllables fading from the plastic

bracelet they have yet to
cut from your wrist, the letters

broken from the outset
the impression left

by the exhausted printer
at Admissions further

blurred by nocturnal sweats.
You lie unclaimed

on a gurney pushed to one side
of the isolation ward where you

waited out your final hours
back and thighs tender

with bedsores attended to
gently, though you were barely

aware or awake, your body
stripped of everything

but a pyjama jacket
and tubes exchanging

sweet stupor for wastes.
You might have looked

through them to the ceiling
so far off, outside

the reach of whatever
vision you had, not always

apprehending cracked plaster
could not forever hold back

the clouds or their leaden descent.
The results came back negative

months ago and already I am
starting not to remember

the briefs you wore that night
only how your body cast

them off, how it welcomed me
inside you in the middle

of the few hours I knew you
how it seemed to have nothing

to protect, so in a hurry
as it rode me, so unconnected

to your brain with its clouds
so dispersed I did not see

them settle until too late
your body riding the unfocused

eye of my own storm
the condom I slipped on

belatedly a windsock
I filled full force and then

the wind dropped
and then

you told me, your bed
adrift and anchorless

in the doldrums without
compass or horizon.

The results came back negative
years ago and already

I am beginning not to remember
your hands or the way

they touched me, how they so
casually joined with mine or how

exactly
I came to be afraid.

The orange body bag I am sure
awaits each one of us is

one-size-fits-all, contains any
weather without effort, zips

open and closed over you
irreversibly from the outside.

Case History

there is a need, sometimes, for clarity, otherwise the heart
which they say is neither male nor female, too freely associates

the body preoccupied with such a vortex of near particulars
it dreams its own country where exiles trade in the fitful

custom of desire — meanwhile the hand held out in love is delicate
but the sad unlacquered nails are bitten to the quick, the boy told

almost since birth he was altogether otherwise so soon beginning
despite what they had taken from him, to remember himself

remembering even today shoulders he caught once in the mirror
squared under a dress whose torn hem his mother lovingly repinned

*

what was taken from him they said is what made her and would
make her so, without clarification — not necessarily one who

would grow to be desirable or beautiful but one who might
love and adopt, when the time comes, should she, despite all

else she might have longed for, conceive of wanting a child of her
own — a life of certain particulars only clarity could ever make

for her; it would be, they said, otherwise too late for him, every
thing too quickly answered before she could have questions

*

for him there was never any question, for him clarity, so-called
was not absent but taken before he could remember, if only

by accident — the current, he now knows coursing too harshly
through some instrument used to untighten his constricted

7-month-old foreskin, 'clarity' in its entirety burned to near 'ablation'
before it 'necrosed' and they 'sloughed' it 'off' but like his 'monozygotic

XY twin' down at the gene level the variables of X and Y still plotted
the same ardent trajectory otherwise rising exponentially between

the spread legs of the graph, the particular line he would come
to trace, the nerve to do so opening through him centrally

at puberty despite whatever they plotted to subtract, despite any
'contingencies' they would have, in all certainty, attempted to add

*

what they have taken from him he knew early on in his heart
is not some thing otherwise consequent — what makes him

sexy is the brain, its ecstatic rush finally reassigned to him
hypodermically, helping him to grow a light beard and chase

after girls he took to with such confidence, taking out the very
ones who before never once thought he was ever in any way

one of them, in whom at last they found no ambiguity
liking the particular cut of his jeans and how he was remade

to fill them in ways he had so long ago began longing for, liking
his open-necked shirts, the muscled body he still trains and does

not conceal despite the soft line of his jaw and the scarring
and all else leftover it is now too late to ever take away

*

for him it is not that the body clarifies, though he knows it
sometimes reveals more than it hides, it is just his sons make

him a father purely by what he does for them, the hockey games
he watches them play at the local arena all through the cold winters

of childhood no one else could understand perfectly like him —
what they have he cannot take from them, even if he tried to

the Y of the men their mother coupled with her X he cannot hope
to shelter them from the otherwise surprising interior weather

of whatever in particular has been left them — instead all he wants is
for each boy to stand in the eventual eye of his own storm, enter

the country no one can claim for him as completely each one
gives himself to the private transformative legacies of lightning

Escher

One thing becomes another.

Two boys grow up
grow apart, live in different cities
day and night cleaving in two, clouds of geese overhead

migrating in opposed directions
sun- or moonlight moulting from their wings
and mirrored across the dark, rain-slicked roofs of slate

as one of us rises
from bed while the other sleeps
goose down from our pillows tangled in our hair

like herring in the nets
of trawlers setting or heaving anchor in oceans
where the rivers below our windows empty, uncoiling like endless

opalescent snakes swallowing
their tails somewhere beyond the circle limit
of the horizon, an infinite labyrinth of fields spread in shrinking

multiples past the eye's dawn- or dusk-lit rim while the backwash
of high tide thrums far upstream against warehouse
quays like blood lured through

veins to the heart, its own circle limit collapsing
inward as memory spirals down a vortex
of expanding

particulars, which, with every tighter downward turn, more
minutely blur, dizzying the flesh aging in the arms
of those who love us, blind

weary flesh later sitting by itself to read the identical
books of Escher prints we gave each other
loosening with knives

those pages now swollen shut, the handstitched bindings silty
from the flood that leaks through the shale and mortar
of our shallow basements.

Ebb and flow overtook us.

Luna

Assembling the platform in the moonlight
they named the tree 'Luna.'
— www.lunatree.org

Up here, among the limbs of a redwood, the living.
Among limbs, the lover's body, one with the tree adrift

in the twilight gloom drifting in from the coast, a giant inside
the forest's red wall of coastal air, banks of condensing

airy exhalation rolling in from open sea —
the windy littoral unseen from up here on an open-air

platform, windblown and almost 200 feet
high among the blowing limbs, a literal cold

and limber platform built for protest from moonlight
in moonlight for the living to live on

so the tree may live on, beyond these near
lightless, clear-cut years, the tree already

torn by centuries, lightning, and fire, its bark
welling tears behind a thousand-year fan

of a thousand expansive greens, towering
courtesan of the greenwood, needles sheared

needlessly from their follicles by the jarring
less far-off roar of approaching loggers

the approaching machinery held back by the groundfast
of the living, who each tree-sit alone, upheld here

by a platform, its small lonely perimeter become
life itself, discourse met with bare feet refusing

conversation with the earth, anorexic, dedication fused
to a kind of earthly hunger made to sustain more

than one body, visionary, kind, only some say mad
St. Joan listening to the tree's voice, to its body

the recluse mind voicing grace through agile feet
wed to graceful limbs in moonglow and fog, sun

and darkness, which, sunless, is sometimes not
wind-shorn darkness but stars, the wind

speaking starlight through the body to the world.
The final word: *Luna*; the first word: *Beloved*.

II

Venture too far for love . . . and you renounce citizenship in the country you've made for yourself. You end up just sailing from port to port.

— Michael Cunningham

In a Station of the Tongue

the Métropolitain breaks through the surface

and the sun-blue Seine flows ever westward

shining damp leaves of the plane trees lifting

their breeze-roughened faces to speak in light

as the train slides forward while I sit back

ease into the slipstream of some sensation

heady flash of summer sun among the leaves

then sudden darkness when we pull below

into Place d'Italie, the station of the Métro

where so long ago I took my first steps down

to the tongue, my estranged sad familiar, this

underground platform I might have come to

by hazards I am unconscious of, this transfer

point so unquittable all journeys elsewhere

seem suspect, no more than ill-fated journeys

of departure, but stepping down to this *place*

for the first time in the flesh, I sense I have

been arriving here always — today on the Day

of the Assumption, Paris celebrants radiating

from the Tuilleries into the Champ de Mars

very few more than vague about the Virgin

or her ascent beyond such an infinitely slow

clearing haze of azure and cirrus while I step

down here, the Métro at last delivering me

from le Cimetière du Père Lachaise, the final

station where the honoured dead one by one

have wordlessly disembarked — Alfred de Musset

Guillaume Apollinaire Gertrude Stein Marcel

Proust — their graves the turned soiled pages

of a thumbed-through gazetteer of the tongue

I picked my way through all morning, never

wholly fluent, the intersecting and divergent

paths through the unkempt shrubbery no less

snarled than chance lines of disordered text

networks worn and written down by visitors

with notebooks and cameras come in search

of deathless alexandrines, though unlike

others there today, I cruised the paths alone

however much I'd felt myself to be among

them, eyes meeting or not, regarding statues

Héloïse and Abélard long prostrate on a bed

of stone above remains theirs by reputation

marble bodies never touching, hands folded

in prayer on stilled breasts, a marriage made

in heaven though they were forced to live

apart, theirs the paradigm of love requited

the missives they sent each other for so long

now among the roots of the tongue, a tongue

transcribed on paper, reflected upon then

changed, its solitary arts a record of solace

and entrapment inside the mouth, words

wanting out, this poem to be revised later

after I ascend from the station to the *place*

above, its closed circle of park and fountain

its statue honouring victors of some Italian

campaign in Tunisia, this place, this civic

square (or circle) where I first came to learn

something of the tongue, the clumsy tongue

in my mouth then without words from 'here'

unschooled, except by intuition, in nuances

of sounds put to desires by tongues other

than my own, starting with the inarticulate

locutions taught to me by a boy up the street

(who, moaning, stuck his tongue in my ear)

and with *la famille Thibeault,* the very model

of love's decorum — *un bon homme sa femme*

et leurs deux petits — a sociable family unit

their apartment in my brand-new grade-six

reader overlooking where I'm now stood still

blinded by sun outside the entry to a station

of the Métro, simultaneously in situ at Banff

Trail Elementary, a sweet, sunny, suburban

school in the Alberta foothills, the birthplace

of how I came to speak the tongue they have

long spoken here, my voice not immaculate

its back highway west rising into rangeland

and the Rocky Mountains, dropping eastward

to God knows where — here perhaps — though

such would never have been my assumption

back then, so imminently before adolescence's

rash embarkations, its many essentialisms

some say should not have, but did lead me to

loving men — *même les beaux gars français*

de mon propre pays — their love always

about how I would use their tongue, never

about how our tongues joined, love finally

expressed as a desire for separation and true

abandon inside some vast snowed-in country

of their own — *ton pays, comme on dit, c'est*

l'hiver — where they wanted to dwell all alone

in the purity of the verb while I only had need

or so I thought, of a room with uncurtained

west-facing windows to let in wet coastal air

coffee, some used books, a thesaurus, a desk

and single bed where I could speak in tongues

any tongue at all, but such wants and men

came later, coming in the far federal capital

where I live tongue-tied now, their fluid

ephemeral love staining the very thin sheets

of my unmade heart, the times we made love

so indelible I am here, there, and elsewhere

and here, *only,* for the very first time — 'here'

the leaf-glazed quartier where I came to learn

something of their tongue before I had need

to, and ever since seem to have used or been

used by its men badly, now speaking with no

comfort my flaccid vocabulary of *épiceries*

and *boulangeries,* this *place* a spoked wheel

blurring, tree-lined avenues spun from traffic

circles all across a city where like-hearted

tongues intertwined centuries ago to become

a country, cutting out the awkward tongues

of others, their speech dissonant to their own

the state at last become Paris and not Paris

heart and wasteland, its diaspora a thinning

nebula of cast-off words, widely drifting —

this *place* a place of historic pasts and eternal

presents, my own and others, the verb tenses

not unlike the dead who are with us always

though by now I have learned what the living

speak here is not the language — nor is Paris

the city — of love, as I was once led to believe

my tongue dry and silent inside my mouth

Parisian men more foreign to me than I am

to them, speaking to me in Berlitz with such

efficient complacent distance, if they speak

to me at all, so dead am I to them they may

as well inter me long before my time in Père

Lachaise like Oscar, mine like his a local

death, or so it would seem, and the sole way

to become a citizen, however damned, of this

very sacred ground, though what is left to mark

my presence and passing will not be defaced

reverentially like his — "AND ALIEN TEARS

WILL FILL FOR HIM / PITY'S LONG BROKEN

URN. / FOR HIS MOURNERS WILL BE OUTCAST

MEN / AND OUTCASTS ALWAYS MOURN." —

though this morning under the fading stars

a Brazilian who spoke such flawless French

as *langue seconde* stopped me near l'Hôtel

de Ville and took me home to Montmartre

his tongue in my mouth, his cock a tongue

speaking deep inside me in syllables too raw

and subtle to be local patois, as sunrise

drenched Sacré-Coeur with the sweetest nacre

only to burn it off by the afternoon, my body

so sticky with sweat he did not tongue off

but, rhapsodic, I have not washed all day

head emptied and flesh torn by the journey

he made through my body, a fast commuter

train so overcrowded with memory and

desire run underground into my outcast arms

he electrified me between stations, liberating

my rhythmic noisy iambs, our conjoined

tongues without dialect, poignancy unwound

between the walled banks of the Seine as it

convolutes in ever more sinuous westward

arcs away from Paris, to conjoin its silty

voyelles with whatever is precipitous, au

courant and unsound in the English Channel

Light Paralysis

by myself among bright distracted crowds
caught moving among the echoes of the old
library the high walls of Trinity all summer
cannot keep out, today I have made a start at
compiling my own *Book of Kells*, not to tell
truths, but to write of how imperfectly I have
come to know them, my writing hand sadly
numb, the ulna nerve once nicked by chance
shards of glass slivering under the pale skin
of my wrist, window breaking, fist reaching
outside a spasm of visionary rage that even
now won't come clear, desires fragmenting
bloodstained, memory a phantasm of lost
feeling not completely animating my index
finger and thumb as I bluntly grip this pen
making notes I will no doubt mistrust about
the scriptorium where celibate, deft, ninth
century tonsured monks worked, copying out

the *Book of Kells* in drafty, window-lit rooms

in a monastery, its precise location remaining

lost in mist — perhaps in the house of the holy

order whose sonorous bell-like name it bears

or on Iona, a small rocky islet off the wind

shorn coast of Scotland (the gentle syllabic

kiss of its name the Hebrew word for 'dove')

the monks losing themselves in the grinding

of pigment and preparing vellum, the imprint

of the frail spinal columns of slaughtered

calves visible in open folios of the sacred

volumes now on display, one leaf turned

every day for the wonderment of the constant

passing crowds in the library's controlled

half-light, barely five turned during the few

short days I have to stay in Dublin, the sole

fragments of the transcribed story I will ever

view (my wingless namesake, John, clasping

a pen cut from the tail feather of a swan not

unlike those the monks centuries later would

have likely grasped, inscribing the gospel

John himself had told of the world to come

bound in red and purple, held in his left hand

the facsimile of his perfect love, a horn filled

with an ink mixed from iron and oak apples

at his feet, every earthly flaw in transcription

or any other infelicitous slip of the hand

marked by the scribes throughout with self

referential sanguine dots, their story lost

inside his story, their signature read from all

these traces, the *Book of Kells* hypothesized

as the sole compelling record left by monks

who long ago wasted into the speechless

paralysis only their graves voice, the surface

of the text undisturbed by all subsequent

interpretations no matter how many leading

letters are insinuated with a whole menagerie

of portents — legions of peacocks, fish, moths

and lions while several unholy faces tempt us

from the scripted hollows and illuminated

mice snatch the host from between the lines

of ink, every single tasty disc a halo caught

in their teeth) what I write in my faulty hand

misshaped, the rough, rushed, unenlightened

transcript of a shy near agnostic who finds

himself travelling all alone in a once religious

country, who walks about Dublin unengaged

in conversation, save when eating yet another

hasty sandwich in Temple Bar or requesting

directions from the lovely, local, lighthearted

men espied while browsing books of modern

Irish poetry at Waterstone's, men with hands

I would like to massage me asleep one night

between taking pictures from Parnell Square

to St. Stephen's Green in the light rain or sun

the Liffey crossed by the Ha'penny Bridge

the river's murky, almost still reptilian flow

impressed by the faintest metallic twilight

glimmers it copies of the bridge's single arch

catapulting in stasis from bank to bank, quays

where thousands cheer on young men and old

in the Liffey Swim, betting on the trained

and fading who race the serpentine currents

to Dublin Bay, as painted by Jack B. Yeats

his canvas of the swim hung off and on since

the early 30s at the National Gallery of Ireland

across from Merrion Square — the *Book of Kells*

undercurrent in every detail I have observed

wandering exhausted from room to room

through ascending gyres of Irish art, spirals

etched into what is fished out of the sodden

peat drowning the Irish with such a deep

subconscious, Bronze-Age lunulae and toncs ornate with snakes and chevrons luminescent yet static inside polished cases ranged around the National Museum beside the hammered relics of a later golden faith — how all things become hypnotic — every predatory Viking raid somehow sailing past the worn, venerated uniforms of those long, never-to-be-forgotten independence struggles and out the door distant O'Connell Street rebuilt but still scarred by 1916's Easter Rising, intervening streets lined with monuments to executed patriots, each cast face recalling some darkly illuminated saint, their brass plaques I read walking to the DART station, the Martello tower where Joyce set several of the early pages of *Ulysses* a reflective commuter-train ride away in Sandycove, the walls of the tight

turning steps to the roof damp to the touch
salty sunswept affinities of the bay still not
experienced fully by the time I find myself
listening to a poet read something she calls
"Bog of Moods," vertiginous rhythms of mid
life in this ancient city opening in rings about
me, late sun pooling around the filled chairs
at the Writers Centre a day before my flight
away, my hand, numb with feeling, unequal
to her delicious miasmic account, my prose
never as textured as the thin washes of ink
the monks had overlaid to trick the future
into sensing lucent depth, sainted faces lined
with *auripigmentum*, eyes holding our gaze
beseeching us across centuries whose shape
the isolated monks could not have guessed
the beauty of their message still enrapturing
these pages, however many ways the story

they tell, and how they tell it, can be lost (all

frames of human understanding any window

of stained glass made from haphazard rosy

fragments and bathed with blinding light

those caught in its shattering glare not able to

express how it articulates their lives within

the shadows or the love they have forsworn

or squandered) the *Book of Kells* incomplete

Christ's solitary passion missing, the page

reserved for its illustration achingly blank

but not the promise of eternal life the text

portends for believers on this or any island

unlike the small stories the rest of us barely

fathom or write out in full, the paralyzing

weight of desire, when felt outside love, spun

into images too tenebrous to apprehend alone

Eye Country

the colour of your eyes, I can't remember

grey or blue, the colours of the windswept

bay in sunlight or fog during the changeable

days just before we met, I can't remember

but due to this lazy eye of mine and its well

cast twin, I have never been a stranger to

vision and its deviations, how like the body

the eyes can wander, moving from place to

face, how I never sense their drift until men

I talk to point this out, ask after the import

of my gaze, so askance it appears I have

grown bored with them, am looking over

their left shoulders when I think I am

meeting their eyes head on, intense irises

sometimes blue, sometimes grey, but slowly

more quizzical as they ponder what beyond

them I might be focused on, their anxiety

shouldered and squared against whatever it

is I happen to see in the haphazard, hazy

skyline of a city cut out like a Potemkin

village before some horizon, San Francisco

in this case, so askew we delay awhile

longer on Marina Blvd near the yacht club

and the Palace of Fine Arts, my back turned

to a fog-infused Golden Gate Bridge, the far

destination of our walk, not ready to face

what might never link us while we attempt

to know each other and how we — or anyone

else — come to see ourselves as men, as one

country in this city of fucking and shopping

of vistas and fog — some man I encountered

before I met you in the dark at the Midnight

Sun on 18th near Noe Street, and like most

we didn't have much time, the two of us

strangers from far cities we too soon must

depart for, leaving the next day or the next

two briefly visionary men who would find
themselves standing side by side along some
outside wall and apart from the beautiful
who were a tangle of garter snakes entwined
on the dance floor, but what I remember is
not your eyes but your gaze, peripheral but
gentle, your whole body a look you turned
ever so slightly toward me as you leaned
against the wall and I inclined in unison
toward you, skewed eyes askance, my hips
angling toward you, toward your laconic
very warm, dark-browed gaze, a presence
shorter than I am, dressed so simply in black
jeans and a navy — or was it charcoal — polo
shirt, a button undone at the neck — and how
tight it looked — I knew even how I would
ease it slowly up your torso over your head
later on, much later, but first we kissed, lips

opening without any reserve to each other

letting in tongues, and they spoke freely

your thigh pressed against me as your face

turned up to mine in the corner by the bar

music cycling in our veins and the night air

till we walked out of the disco's dry icy mist

onto Castro and down to the traffic lingering

all along Market Street as it cut diagonally

through the city and into the dark beyond

what eyes can ever hope to see in the fog

settling onto Twin Peaks, hands trying not

to link, walking past shut neighbourhood

boutiques and newsstands, past the blue

café where after the hours I whiled away

browsing and buying in the vintage clothing

and antiquarian bookshops along the breath

arresting sudden falls and rises of the views

I took countless photos of, too few of them

ever to turn out to be what I saw, blocking

shot after shot from several hilltops along

Fillmore and Divisadero between Haight

Ashbury's faded psychedelia and the oxygen

thin opulence of Pacific Heights, the busy

precipitous streets dropping away on either

side while I trained my throwaway autofocus

Instamatic northward onto the bay's grey

blue — or was it green — I found myself alone

and eating, one last time lingering over café

pork chops, mashed red potatoes, and yellow

beans, the window's thick glazing doubling

me as I looked out onto the street, stared

solitude in the eye, or did I look over its left

shoulder — who can ever tell — the growing

clarity of what was captured there obscuring

passersby while night deepened, while I ate

listening to young men whisper knee-to-knee

in other booths, their quotidian, half-grasped

conversations staying with me, their languid

smiles and casually conscious dress caught

in my pale reflection, suggesting unlike me

they were citizens of this place, their quiet

eucalyptus-lined back avenues we trespassed

walking along to 24 Henry where I was to stay

one final night, our chests and loins so relaxed

as we released each other from our clothes

such liberties only temporary, for you could

not stay long, your pale outline indistinctly

drawn against the dark as I watched you

dress and leave, the no man's land we had

occupied to make our own, its terrain fixed

by a disposable sightless flash of orgasm's

flare, where afterward you found space for

a kind of asylum in the depths of my arms

harbouring there, an immigrant ship dropping

anchor in the fogged-in bay with just time

enough for boarding and disembarkation

under the lighthouse's blank wandering eye

the male body spontaneous and free-form

and more of a country here than elsewhere

whose nationals by their presence give

refuge, though the border left to cross is

never one solely of vision and desire —

many may gain entrance but not all can stay

III

For "to read" a country is first to perceive it according to the body and memory, according to the memory of the body.
— Roland Barthes

Book of the Southwest

Sunrise, Grand Canyon

We stand on the edge, the fall
into depth, the ascent

of light revelatory, the canyon walls moving
up out of

shadow, lit
colours of the layers cutting

down through darkness, sunrise as it
passes a

precipitate of the river, its burnt tangerine
flare brief, jagged

bleeding above the far rim for a split
second I have imagined

you here with me, watching day's onslaught
standing in your bones — they seem

implied in the record almost
by chance — fossil remains held

in abundance in the walls, exposed
by freeze and thaw, beautiful like a theory

stating who we are
is carried forward by the X

chromosome down the matrilineal line
recessive and riverine, you like

me aberrant and bittersweet, and losing
your hair just when we have begun

to know the limits of beauty, you so
distant from me now but at ease

in a chair in your kitchen, pensive, mind
wandering away from yesterday's *Times*, the ink

rubbing off on your hands, dermatoglyphic
and telltale, but unread

on the chair arms after you
had pushed yourself to your feet such

awhile ago, I'd say, for here I am
three hours behind you, riding the high

Colorado Plateau as the opposing
continental plates force it over

a mile upward without buckling, smooth
tensed, muscular fundament, your bones yet

to be wrapped around mine —
this will come later, when I return

to your place and time, I know it, you not
ready for past or future, our combined

bones so inconsequent yet
personal, the geo

logic cross
section of the canyon dropping

from where I stand, hundreds
millions of shades of terra cotta, of copper

manganese and rust, the many varieties of stone —
silt, sand, and slate, even "green

river rock," a rough misidentified
fragment of it once unknowingly

dropped when I was a boy into my as of yet un
settled sediments by a man who tried

to explain how slowly the Earth meta
morphosed from my meagre

Wolf Cub's collection of rocks, his sheer
casual physicality enough to negate

all received wisdom, my body voicing its immense
genetic imperatives, human

geology falling away
into a

depth I am still unprepared for
the canyon cutting down to

the great unconformity, a layer
so named by the lack

of any fossil evidence to hypothesize
about and date such

a remote time by, at last no possible
retrospective certainties, what a

relief, your face illegible
these words when I began not what I had

intended to say — something new about
the natural dynamic between

earth and history, beauty and art —
but you are my subject, unavoidable

and volatile, the canyon
floor a mile from where I objectively

stand taking photos I will later develop of
the ripe, trans

formative light on these surreal
buttes to show you on the surface

how beautiful and diverse
and unimportant our time together

or with anyone else
really is —

Against the Current of the Virgin

Now that we have entered Zion
it is time to step from the bank

into the shallows and wade
staff in hand, upward against

the current of a river driven to carry
us downstream or hold us here, pull one

or both of us
under in some eddy uncoiling

in wait at the base of a cliff
our destination not the river's

source — only the skilled try to
reach it, for to approach

is to wade back through
time — how we became who we are

summarized in the fluid
layers of rock by persistent flood

the details smooth, partially exposed
haphazard, rough, a journey

we are told each must orienteer
alone, the thigh-deep cold

water suggestive
however, of the glacier, tasting

of the cavity where it loiters, wearing
down the mountain, releasing

trace elements
as we continue wading in

through the present with no real
end in mind, at first you

then I leading the way as we
stumble over

submerged rocks, one winding many
steps behind the other from shoal

to sandbar, through slow and fast
moving water, unable to avoid

chest-deep sinkholes and the occasional
long portage, knowing we will go only

as far as we can, this brief upward
journey for whatever distance something

we appear to share, though right now
we seem to be drawn so far

apart, several deep channels between us
the mercurial current and these walls

ascending 3000 feet, only to darkly
narrow, the porous lime

stone leaching blinding
shades of light until one

or the other calls
a halt, our backs

turning against the origins
the river aspires from, to see

what little we've passed through
from a different vantage, our faces

like the canyon unexpectedly
unfamiliar in the slow rising

darkness as we repick our way
over shelves of rock, neither of us

certain who is leading, in sync
only with the current, its inexorable

dangerous tumble downward
over splintered

boulders, uprooted trees and through
twisted gorges until one takes

the other's hand one last time for
balance, the anxious

solitude of the journey upstream
nothing to the unrecognizable

proscription of the descent to where
we might know ourselves again, the walls

of limestone lighting
our way yet blocking

the sun at turns
transparent and opaque

while the Virgin River we step from
cleansed yet dirty

roars onward in pious radiance
unrepentant and misnamed.

Disappearance of the Anasazi

The car broke down
we thought, in Cortez

Colorado, the engine not turning
over when you depressed

the clutch and then
mysteriously

five hours ago
it started, the clutch

depressed by some sweet
mechanic, the tuned

machine of his body
for a moment behind our wheel

and then we were gone
the suggestive

spread of his thighs as he teased
the brakes a persistent heat

mirage we drove toward
but never reached while our car

laboured over twisting
blacktop freshly laid

into Mesa Verde
the park gates well in

from the highway turnoff
the time we had left

to spend unequal to the lay
of the land, the many fingers

of the mesa splayed into barren
plains we had trouble

conceiving, looking hazily
down arroyos widened below

and away from us as we stood
among the excavations

at each site the young clean
shaven rangers breaking

our concentration with the facts
of how the Anasazi left

the mesa top
for the numberless

fissures in its wind-gouged
striated face, built multi

storied communal dwellings
with bricks of mud and straw

the materials for them
along with food and water

they shifted on their backs
from above, footholds cut

so cunningly into the cliffs
when the untoward started

down with the wrong foot
they would several holds later

fall to astonished deaths
each ranger's lean

shadow distending across the flesh
toned walls a people

civilized for a century, then
abandoned, the reasons

not apparent to
archaeologists who crave

evidence to excite a theory
they feel comfortable believing

without prejudice
the disappearance

of the Anasazi never meant to be
a breakdown in their logic

evidence I weighed, driving
away from the Temple

of the Sun, the actuality
of our being here

more telling than any speculative
frame of those who unearth

effects
their veneration

of objectivity more
important than the object —

me assuming this in all arrogance
as we looked away from each

other blankly, the shared
moment hard

to focus on when all of us
are vacancies, craven, carried

forward until desire peters
out and blurs, failure

seen reflected in traces
where none exists

until the heat exhausted
us and we grew

afraid the car would strand us
in the park, but it coughed

to a start
and we disappeared.

A Restaurant Guide to Santa Fe and Region

We eat in less than perfect silence
having once had too much

to say, not knowing what little
skill it would take to map everything

lying between us — deceptive
nondescript terrain we now less

carelessly transgress
liquoring ourselves

instead with conversation à la carte
such a waste

when words are scarce
as water this far

south
all the distances we've travelled

the effort and expense
the fine clothes brought to fit in

at the Eldorado Hotel for breakfast
or the Santa Café for an aperitif

the sun sinking red and rare
and earlier than we are

used to, the air cool
the courtyard heaters unable

to blunt the chill on this bottle
of Napa Valley wine, but we have

nothing to complain about, already
nostalgic for Arizona and the spare

star-eyed spaces
we've left half seen

behind us, simple truck-stop fare
exchanged for these exotic

book-length menus, their civilized
example unglimpsed in the tame

Wild-West, film-set
landscapes of Monument Valley

or in the flakes of turquoise
worked with silver I bought from Chief

Yellowhorse at one of his trinket stands
strung like beads along the highway

from Tuba City to Gallop
the ring blackening

my baby finger
sagebrush rolling to a photo

finish from the ditches
as we blew past the crass

Native-run casinos down Route 66
looking for Nat King Cole

and Eartha Kitt —
we always cash in too late

the motels of the 1950s closed
or torn down and replaced

with something more upscale
where prawns are steamed

with gingered rice and wrapped
in banana leaf, the stars

awarded restaurants increasing
as the plateau ascends

toward Taos and Santa Fe
tables deftly arranged

inside bylaw-mandated
cactus-fringed, halvah-coloured

pueblo-style haciendas
what Georgia O'Keeffe called

Santa Fake
and slowly the tables

have come to turn on us
our plates turning

cold no matter what restaurant
we pick as we carp

and dish each other
love cooked up by a need

for sustenance we cannot sustain
despite the flavoured

oils and spices we indulge in
the vegetables seeming

to delight us less, blue corn
and organic squash cultivated

on irrigated land without
reference to

the Sangre de Cristo Mountains
looking dryly down upon the city

their creeks cascading only
during spring flood

otherwise negligible tributaries
of the Rio Grande, intense

and forgettable as any
vagrant road-trip passion.

Plateaus of the Eternal

The permit to take pictures
at Taos Pueblo is tagged

to my camera, with its seeming
wide-angled perspectives and quick

shift adjustments you take
little interest in, though

you will no doubt enjoy
the results of what I capture

on film long after we separate
you to buy Indian flatbread

and me to record the transaction
from the other side of the sacred

river dividing North from South
House, the water still so pure

no one may drink of it save
those born at or descended from

the source high in the mountains
Blue Lake ceded back at last

by the government to the Red
Willow people, their own

(translated) name, not
the one the Spanish

conferred and the anthropologists
soon codified, the cosmos

or what remains of it, once again theirs
within the bounds of this reservation

though we may intrude for a price
your back to me in the frame

of the bakery door cut this
century into the half-millennium

thick mud-and-straw walls
of a pueblo advertised for its timeless

authenticity despite the cracked
linoleum floors, the electricity, the late

model cars sheltered under roof-high
racks still used to dry corn —

details I attempt to avoid as I block
each one of my shots, zooming

in from such a distance
no one will notice what truly

is here, and sometimes I fail
you being a hard man to isolate

from everyone else who has come with
hungers to restore, self-contained

and diligent, fingering pottery
on a table outdoors, its beauty

you can only respond to viscerally, not
judge the worth of, unlike the imperfect

man I tried later to love
who did not come to the Southwest

with us — or did he — a presence whom
in retrospect it seems I have fleshed

out to replace you, reflecting on how
we drove across a desert, its history

in each retelling I can't convey
the sense of, his absence your silence

while you browse through
the guidebooks as I switch wistful

gears from one state to the next
the mesas we speed past

revealing fossils whose nomenclature I am
yet to recall, though I have no one

to fault, the rock holding them continuing
to erode as I write this, shaky and still

shifting the facts almost a year later
unable to construct the imagined

life he would refuse me soon enough
the two of you becoming one

man in the treacherous
plateaus of the eternal

present I travel without destination
from one day to the next, the differences

between us, between the two of you
dropped from the narrative

though in the pictures I take
of one man buying bread

when developed, three discretely
blessed men against the many

storied pueblo are revealed
restoration not about what museums

scrape away to betray pure lines
of structure, but an accounting

of multiples, of how we expose
accreted layers of haphazard

time simultaneously, without apology
in the pursuit of desire, who we are

more than what we are named
more than what we name in ourselves.

Eschatology of Skin

We are all interchangeable
yet hopelessly unique

leaning against the wall
among the shadows

of the Drama Club
where Santa is at last

completely fey, the fickle
Native and local Latino

boys moving among unoriginal
inhabitants who come briefly

to town with drop-dead
sculpted looks to study art

but instead find each other, here
posing under coloured lights

conflated in the floor's mirror tile
unlike us who spend only

one unselfconscious night
between the suspiciously clean

sheets of the Desert Chateau
before moving on, one motel

room indifferent to the next
when compared

to the men we did not bring
back with us, our dreams

the extra blankets
folded and frayed and left

unused on the top
shelf of every room's empty

closet, though, at the 8000 feet
we have risen to, the thinning

air is seldom cold, whatever
chill evaporating in the dawn

light as we drive from canyon rim
to canyon rim, pulling away

from a motel by the artificially
pent-up waters of Lake Mead

our destination some other
town cited in *Fodor's*

Gay Guide to the U.S. Southwest
thumbnail city plans spreading

hazy grids, the street names
recurrent, the dance clubs

saunas, and cafés not easily
found, risible, irritating

as the grit lifted from and eroding
the land, obscurely beautiful

transients lounging on bar stools
against whose cagey, smooth

shaven chests we contemplate
forgetting what we can

not wear away, the hurt
in your eyes, the confusion

in mine, interchangeable but
not unique, the miles

ahead, distances we seem
to travel to get

to the end of
only, the network of worn

down highways we follow
intricate and bare

as the cracks in a lake bed
drying up, only to miss

the turnoff to a Comfort Inn
where we might at last hold

someone in our arms, a man
who is every or no other

man we have ever
held, the demarcations

between heaven and hell
subtly hued as the layers

of dust hardened into the great
backward-looking ages

of the Earth, one man told
what might have been

said to another, unmaking both
into one and none, this terrain

embracing through wind
and water all prior

landscapes coinciding
here, no more sacred

than whatever kivas two
bodies, joining, make —

creosote mixed with clay —
'x' and 'x' and 'x'

lovers whose names come
unbidden to our lips as we kiss

some man unforetold
in imagination or in the flesh

our own names rising to the lips
of other men while we sit

unconscious in the car puzzling over
directions at dusk while we transect

the laconic mauve breath
lessness of the Painted Desert

only later to expire deeply far
from each other on some crowded

floor, its patina rainbowed
with sweat, the eschatology

of skin oiled by lurid
gels of the strobe, tranced

techno denaturing our blood
its heat drumming in the veins

of changelings uniquely unsteady
on our feet in this afterlife.

Anthropomorphism

At Acoma Pueblo
I have never been more

unstable, the sky in tumult
as we climb the road to the brim

of the mesa the village
is cobbled over, the narrative

of our trip in fragments
the unruly

elevations we've crossed
the fluid, laid-down

sequential seams of time
convulsed, cut

through, tumbled
worn away, precipitated

reversed
the most recent

depression settled one
thousand feet below

beautiful and on the surface
calm, indifferent

to whom in their aridity
the shattered

voices exposed in the blood
lit layers are speaking

and for whom, where
and when, the facts

the guide blandishes no
more telling than the mud

washed houses circling
the plateau on the street

she trails us down, though
elsewhere we've learned

beyond the four compass points
two other directions offer

solace in the Southwest
the viscera split

open countless times by
sudden canyons

we never tire of gazing
down into, fissures

in the Earth we have all
come from (such anthropo

morphism) to move up
toward the sky, stars

caught in grandiose
shifts as we form

them into whatever patterns
we aspire to, life caught

midway between
on

plateaus, in body and imagination
until it is time —

Acoma not what I'd hoped for
at one remove through the eyes

of Willa Cather
death come to her narrative

in unresolvable tropes I can barely
contemplate, nowhere to be

found the martyred peach trees
she describes withering

in the churchyard, the unmentioned
now Christian dead buried

one above the other in a verticality
unique to this place, hallowed

ground the elders say outsiders
cannot transgress, nor are we

uncondemned to eternal life as we travel
the ups and downs of the disrupted

text this landscape is
on our way to Phoenix

the airport and home
where I will discover certain

bones were never mine to
wrap my own around

for the duration of something
so thin as a sheet

of time, you and I gone quickly
extinct, absence rewriting

past and future, flux
like bodies

of the night sky
waves of sedimentary

light radiating
from far and near stars, the after

math collected in unsound layers —
mendacious, uncarbon-datable

evanescent illuminations —
the heart a refuge

where no story
ever clearly forms.

Sky News

It was a place we did not go, though
the road signs, if we let them, would have

taken us off course, crossing the plateau
between Albuquerque and Flagstaff, ceaseless

terra cotta clouds of grit almost
sweeping us from the interstate, driven

and insentient, the wind unaware
of how it shook us, of how I gripped

the wheel, the loneliness
of my concentration, as I steered

between the gusts, the mountains west
of Flagstaff impossibly celestial

snow falling when we pulled in for coffee
before pressing on, time not sacrificed

to distance, or wherever farther on
we felt we had to go, realizing

too late what we had passed by —
the crater outside town where the meteor

struck, record of one of the smaller
impacts to disturb the countenance

of the Earth, devastating
in its clarity, only a mile across

I am told, and therefore comprehensible
in this landscape, how it came

out of nowhere and did not miss
suggesting, even to the casual

eye how what we can never expect
or aim to ignore, still leaves

its mark — news
from the sky, we should have

watched for it, the whole planet watching
for it, fearful inventories kept of the near

Earth asteroids, networked
telescopes plotting their degrading

erratic orbits, hoping to deflect
disaster or welcome its approach

how it might remake us so completely
unforeseen versions of ourselves

afterward documenting the site
of the collision, the breadth

and unfated depth of its depression
bringing to light unearthly shrapnel still

able, several geologic ages later, to reveal
how it came to be here or any other

suspect signs of life it may have
brought from elsewhere, elusive

yet distracting, while in the immediate
fallout whole categories of phyla

died out, the petrified
hope, the ignored evolutionary

possibilities of leaf and wing
they left behind useless

portents, though the horseshoe
crab grappling up through the layers

sidesteps the trilobite
into what we call the present

— though you (whoever you are
and what I made you) may have

stopped listening (my obsessions
projections into your — or is it my — inner

space) the small impact we had
on each other no more

lasting than any meteor burning up
in-atmosphere, the brilliance

of our brief light
as we drove into the stars

past Flagstaff extinguished
before we had a chance

to notice, leaving no evidence
of its descent except in memory

and this too will fade — love's tiny
universal scale and the uses

to be made of it only a tracker of near
misses can ever predict fully

as I plot the hazy coordinates
of some place whose inevitability

we think this once
we bypassed.

IV

Trudeau's Children

The brown leather trench coat I don't remember
my father wearing strangely
fits me, I am his

body for the first time, this man whose presence
I've long felt to be taller and more
broad-shouldered

than mine could ever be, yet this coat must have fit him
once, its style so unlike how I had grown up to
see him, purchased after I'd left home

years before the stroll Trudeau took through snow falling
in cobwebs onto Ottawa, a lone figure moving past
the Peace Tower, his shadow multiplied

under the street lamps lining Wellington from the Archives
to the Château, the last night in February in the leap
year he chose to leave us — his coat

so like my father's, its executive signature, double
breasted buttons and single vent, its wide
collar up, the belt

knotted loosely, the soft leather uneasy on his shoulders
like a skin about to be shed — I can't fathom
how my father, who still votes

Conservative, could extend his arms into such urbane
sleeves as I've just done, as if into the end
of an era he did not want

to comprehend and could not wait to see the tailored back of
or maybe he guessed its time was already up, the coat
bought on a whim during the down

market interregnum of Joe Who and kept in the belief
he could somehow have it
altered, I can't

imagine, can't see what he saw when he looked
himself over in the showroom
mirror, the cut not

yet retro or even retrospective, lined with the expensive dark
sheen of ambition that recalls the sexy buzz about
a man so unlike our fathers, unmarried

who wore top hats and sandals, who did not sport
a bow tie, who had travelled and foresaw
a future we would read about

in high school, the mirror of history held up
to me as I turn, my father's coat
insouciantly draped

across my shoulders, and I am quite impressed
my Dorian-Gray-like demeanour
not yet completely

gone, though my skepticism must be on drugs, given
the cockeyed figure of a thinking man
in leather it seems

to cut, propositioning in either tongue with capricious eyes
while flirting with the just society, disarmament
fuddle duddle, and Charter rights

Trudeau's coat unable to keep out of the closets of the nation's
bedrooms after all, though it's been awhile
since anyone has tried

it on, though they claim the fiscally more repressed
knockoffs in the stores today are about
the same — look

buy me a drink somewhere and I'll wear this rag and nothing
but, reminisce about the rose never fully
blown in any ideological

lapel — too soon the petals dropped — despite my father
admitting it never fit him well, this coat unlike
us is still in vogue.

Somewhere Marked Farther Down the Lines of Destiny

how to become and remain a country — must it begin with the narrowing
of a river and the inevitable, almost always defensible cliffs that walls are

built upon and then grown far beyond long before they are taken down
though sometimes not, the stone centuries-old gates we pass beneath today

under siege once by an army my forebear led after the unlooked-for death
of Wolfe, the subtle fading colours of the other fallen but opposing general

now backlit dimly at the Musée de l'Amérique française, the thin fabric
of his king's standard immense and unmoved by the wind crystallizing

as it lifts from the ice-riven river, its undercurrent widening at Québec
farther than the eye can foresee into the great estuary whose silver reaches

opened toward Cartier, Champlain, and the British Navy with the same
outspread arms, for what further choice can a river make, the line of destiny

you've read forward only as you followed its faint tracery across my hand
perhaps crossing yours, my body taken into your bed the first night with such

abandon — and wholly culpable, expressing in my build and stance what I fear
had come to be long-held, intensely unconscious habits, the stiff muscles

of my neck warming under your experienced, unfamiliar hands as I gave
myself without thought to a man named after some pope who was sainted

in the years before we were born into what is now a far-off century, wayward
snow slanted into the wind blowing despite the thick archaic walls without

respite off the river and through the city as each night we fall asleep
more entwined, two men in search of the lost country two bodies make

a confederation of sorts, however brief, but hoping to endure alongside
what time assembles here, the ruined city your ancestors rebuilt stone

by stone, the repaired convents and the seminary, the later monuments
to cardinals and foreign queens, lanes lined with surviving, several-storied

houses running up, down, and across the old quarter's disparately pitched
icy inclines, the once cobbled squares overwhelmed by the architectural

styles of successive regimes in conflict, a few declining churches transformed
overnight into museums and libraries, cafés and tourist shops opening, closing

as one-way traffic on Saint-Jean brakes downhill despite layers of salt toward
Simon's on Côte de la Fabrique where we browse the marked-down winter

clothes and *maintenant il est difficile pour moi de ne pas te parler en français
malgré que parfois tu ne me comprennes pas*, the eternal candle on your table

sheltered from every persistent draft by its charred shade of glass, the flame
motionless at the centre of your home in the city's heart where you receive me

as the icebound river does with open arms but, narrowing or widening, unlike
the river you are not indifferent to whom this new invader is and what I bring

All That Enters Must Pass Through —
Love, the Virtual Body, and the Decline of the Nation-State

"the interior has achieved another coup d'état"

This body: its constitution
beyond amendment and spastically tense, the upper
and lower chambers of the heart loud with perpetually ringing

bells and filibusters remembered from the past: my 60s childhood,
premature bedtimes, random Montréal mailboxes blowing
up into the October Crisis, house arrest

after school, and the War Measures Act, *just watch me*
watch reruns of soldiers on Ste-Catherine preempt cartoons
in fast-moving black and white; a few more armchair assassinations

from Pierre Laporte to Kanesatake and the body is pure
instant-on, panicked, the gastric tract
lubricated by spoonfuls

of mineral oil, though less and less sense
of self slips by the body's apparently undefended boundaries
some tight-assed customs officer opening my briefcase with a smirk.

Who knows what anyone's wrongs and rights are anymore, inside or out
but let go and the dollar sinks, all systems borderline
immunodeficient, factories shutting down

and moving south. The body
and its seized-up conveyor belts: economic
depression become somatic, the remotest cells starving

for love, its currency inflated each time we kiss. The text abbreviated
in the flesh. But who has time to read? We watch
the country lose sight of itself.

*

The land we come to is the land we are

: your cheek an unregenerate clear-cut forest
: scalp the tree line receding
: eyes unsmelted ore strip-mined from the almost exhausted shield
: thighs slivers of prairie embedded like shrapnel in exploding suburbs
: ribs caging a discount outlet open 24 hours along some edge-city strip
: hernia scar the pulled-up tracks of a forgotten railroad
: loins the nearby lakes emptying of fish
: your heart a hole endless traffic rips out of the ozone

before it's gone I want to touch the land as it is.

*

Love, you want to leave
and I don't want to

let go. Montréal newspapers
spell your name in the skimmed headlines

an acrostic rubbing off in my hands
as I turn

the pages, sentiment
I can't wash off or away: smeared

toxic inks absorbed by an epidermis letting
things in and not out

living in a federation
its borders we say are not

up for negotiation (no matter how restless
the Natives).

Inside the body, the psyche balances
thyroid and liver, brain and heart, the involuntary

nervous system impartial
unless thrown off

by something not quite withstanding.
In this cold country: Montréal a veritable

city of romance. How I would miss its snow
filled streets and packed

cafés with you gone
its museums suddenly empty and cinemas

recycling untold matinees of your absence.
Or my absence, for I would come

here no longer, unable to revisit
what we have now become, ghosts fitfully

asleep under the icy sheets of economic slowdown.
Once I would have given you

freedom of the city, would have
left my Métro pass and keys locked inside

an apartment leased in both our names before
catching a westbound Voyageur bus

left you to this life, to the divisive
polis at its heart you want to map, but I can't

leave you no matter where we draw
borders we won't discuss.

You are inside of me even when
I am on the outside, my ancestors since

the Plains of Abraham dug deep as compost into
the churchyards of the Eastern Townships.

My kind are taught to contain
ourselves, the imperial flourish

of an irritable bowel almost
Victorian in its habits.

*

All that enters must pass through.
Goods cross into Detroit from Windsor.
All that enters must pass through.
Eros uploaded with the food we eat.
All that enters must pass through.
Praise Gaia for the information highway.
All that enters must pass through.

*

In a 500-channel universe we are still
what we eat: stockpiled mother's
milk, CNN, takeout

pizza, 24-hour
shopping — the body

a network of networks: bloodlines
nerves, and the intestines. Hopelessly

interwoven for what centuries
must feel like, we let ourselves

let go of our limits, forget whatever borders
we did not choose and pick up
speed, our baud

rates pushing against those
of light and infinity until the connection somehow

fails and now, though you are gone, you are everywhere
projected against the blank screen
of my stand-alone

conscience or suspended
in memory. In the virtual, the sewage

of your desire washes through my less-and-less
carbon-based circuitry, your sweet
white noise I call up

repeatedly, all language
a simulation, sentient and magic.

Language heals, not love or medicine. Language is zero
and indivisible. Language lets go
of what it withholds

and gives up nothing
metaphor its viscera and lower colon.

Language is a microchip I collect (picking up
after the virtual cows) and burn
for warmth.

Our bodies speak
in languages we do not comprehend

yet we know who we are, distinct despite
the ether's apparent lack
of borders.

Let us go then, love
let us let go: something always dis or re

connects us to something.
What we singly burn
inside our bodies

joins in loose constellations
frayed networks of light ablur in the wheeling

night skies — the vaporous trails of our opposed
headlights archived for virtual broadcast
long after we race by each

other above
the river, its rank pixelated

flow between the bridge pylons star-crossed if oceanbound —
undercurrents pushing apart eroded
green shores

from whose viewpoints for a nanosecond
we look across to one another, then speed away.

Acknowledgements

I would like to thank the editors of the following publications where some of these poems (sometimes in slightly different forms) have previously appeared:

Capilano Review: "Against the Current of the Virgin," "All That Enters Must Pass Through," "Disappearance of the Anasazi," and "Sunrise, Grand Canyon"
Contemporary Verse 2: "Body Bag" and "Oxygen"
Event: "A Restaurant Guide to Santa Fe and Region"
Fiddlehead: "Phone Lines" and "Prêt-à-Porter"
Grain: "Eschatology of Skin"
The Malahat Review: "Escher," "Hybrid," and "The Living Room"
Poetry Wales: "Somewhere Marked Farther Down the Lines of Destiny"

Some poems also appeared in two limited-edition chapbooks: *Oxygen* (Maxville, Ontario: above/ground press, 1999) and *Shroud* (Ottawa: Viola Leaflets, 1999).

I would also like to thank the following friends for their willingness to act as sounding boards for these poems during their long evolution: Rita Donovan, Robert Gore, Neile Graham, James Gurley, David Jarraway, Penn Kemp, Norma Lundberg, and Blaine Marchand. Thanks also to Martha Sharpe, Adrienne Leahey, Debbie Gaudet, Brian Panhuyzen, and Angel Guerra at Anansi for guiding the book from manuscript to press. Special thanks to Erin Mouré for her engagement with the text in its final stages.

Thanks also goes to the Canada Council for the Arts and the Ontario Arts Council. I would not have been able to complete this book without their financial support in 1999 and 2000.

Notes

The epigraph to "The Living Room" is from P. K. Page's poem, "In Memoriam," from *Hologram* (London: Brick Books, 1994); its final line, which is italicized, is from W. H. Auden's "In Memory of W. B. Yeats." "Bog of Moods," a poem referred to in "Light Paralysis," is by the Dublin poet, Paula Meehan. "Book of the Southwest" opens with an epigraph from Roland Barthes's "La lumière du sud-ouest," an essay in his posthumous *Incidents* (Paris: Éditions du Seuil, 1987); this passage was translated with the assistance of Erin Mouré. The epigraph to "All That Enters Must Pass Through" is from a poem of the same name in my book, *A Poor Photographer* (Victoria: Sono Nis Press, 1981).

All other epigraphs are drawn from *The Bush Garden* by Northrop Frye (Toronto: House of Anansi Press, 1971); *Autobiography of Red* by Anne Carson (New York: Alfred A. Knopf, 1998); *The Farewell Symphony* by Edmund White (New York: Alfred A. Knopf, 1997); and *The Hours* by Michael Cunningham (New York: Farrar, Straus and Giroux, 1998).

Two asides: Northrop Frye's "Where is here?" could be variously resuscitated for contemporary purposes as, for example, "Where is queer?" Jesse Green's equation, $X + X = 0$, from *The Velveteen Father* (New York: Villard Books, 1999), helped focus "Watershed," as did the Earth Day truism, "Gay sex is green sex."

The following poems are dedicated: "Prêt-à-Porter" to Michael MacLennan, "Plasma, Triangles of Silk" to Lynn Wilson, "Escher" to David Young, "Sky News" to Wendy McPeake, and "Trudeau's Children" to Ross Hornby and Miranda Pearson.